BASH STRE
YEARBOOK

The BigHead-master.

Ladybird books are widely available, but in case of
difficulty may be ordered by post or telephone from:

Ladybird Books – Cash Sales Department
Littlegate Road Paignton Devon TQ3 3BE
Telephone 01803 554761

A catalogue record for this book is available
from the British Library

Published by Ladybird Books Ltd Loughborough Leicestershire UK

Introduction

Bash Street School, Bash Street, Beanotown.

Friends, readers, countrymen… welcome to a year in the life of our lovable young rogues, The Bash Street Kids. You may think they're just a lazy bunch of worthless good-for-nothings, but this is not true. In fact they are just shy, misunderstood rascals who like to show their deep respect for their beloved Teacher and myself by playing wicked pranks on us!

We know they don't mean any harm – and don't worry, they've promised me faithfully that this yearbook will be a tribute to their perfect manners and behaviour.

Yours Headmasterly,

The Headmaster

Naaaa! Forget Mr. Bowtie. We're wild, we're free – we can do ANYTHING we want to! We've got coloured pens and sticky tape! This is OUR yeerbook!

To save money, Olive kindly offered to take our photos using her old Box Brownie. She said her photographs were as good as her cooking. Unfortunately, she was right!

Our beloved leaders *Not!*

Headmaster
Our beloved Headmaster
Useless

Teacher
Our beloved Teacher
rotten

Olive
*A rotten cook and
a worse photographer*

Janitor
A genius with a brush

Winston
School cat

Qualifications: ← for being rubbish

Headmaster:	PhD in Advanced Headmastering.
Teacher:	Teacher's Diploma for being Really Clever.
Olive:	GCSE in Woodwork.
	School Dinner Lady by Royal Appointment.
Janitor:	Graduate of Bob's Janitors' School.
Winston:	He's the only cat who asked for the job.

Plan of Bash Street School

Bash Street School is a very happy place where the children learn all sorts of wonderful things like sums, history and spelling. Just to be on the safe side, however, we have to make sure they don't leave before home time.

They can make us go to school, but they can't make us learn!

We conducted a survey to find out the pupils' views of their school. Printed below are the results.

WHAT WE LIKE ABOUT SCHOOL TOP TEN	
1	Going home
2	Going home
3	Going home
4	Going home
5	Going home
6	Going home
7	Going home
8	Going home
9	Going home
10	Going home

WHAT WE HATE ABOUT SCHOOL TOP TEN	
1	Having to go to school
2	Actually going to school
3	Seeing the school bus
4	Getting up in the morning
5	Cuthbert Cringeworthy
6	Teacher
7	Olive's school dinners
8	Sums
9	History
10	Writing stupid lists of 'Top Tens'

Ho, ho! The children like their little jokes! Imagine pretending that they hate going to school!!!

Signed, Teacher.

The only little joke here!

School clubs

It's not all hard sums, history and school dinners at Bash Street.

That's 'cos we don't do any work, and we wont eat school dinners!

This is how the kids have fun…

We have a popular Chess Club…   *rugby is a favourite…*

so are archery…

and lion-taming.

Sport for all!

Once again, Athletico Bash Street won the local football championship, crushing Posh Hill in the final.

In the National Ice Hockey Championship, the Bash Street Flyers narrowly crushed Posh Hill Racers, 98-0.

As usual, our Formation Shark Fishing team was also triumphant.

Of course, we would not have been so successful in these competitions without the invaluable help of the referee – our beloved Headmaster.

BASH STREET
SPACE PROJECT

When Teacher told us we were going to do a class project, he said we were supposed to do something of great benefit to mankind. So we are — we're going to send him to Mars!

The launch is very simple:

1. Fatty eats three tons of cream cakes.

2. Fatty is lowered onto skool roof by helicopter.

3. A rocket made from squeezy bottles and sticky tape is put onto one end of a see-saw.

4. Fatty jumps onto the other end of see-saw.

5. Teacher lands on Mars.

As you can see we're using solid fuel boosters — Fatty and a bag of cream cakes. We haven't worked out how to bring Teacher back. That's his half of the project!

Our heroes

It may be hard to believe, but Bash Street School has a proud history and hundreds of famous former pupils. Every year, many of them make the happy pilgrimage to visit the humble school where their talent was first recognised. Here are just a few:

Teacher's hero is himself!

Teacher loves Teacher

Rick Handsome

Swoon! Rick is so handsome!!!

Toots

Arnold Splatzenegger

Arnie is brilliant! I bet Teacher used to be scared of him!

Danny

Nigel Swot

I could really help Nigel improve his chess.

Bighead →

Cuthbert

Paul Gasket

I think it's great that someone as fat as Paul Gasket can be a football star!

Fatty

Sulky Brogan

Sulky would make a better dinner lady than Olive.

'Erbert

A dinosaur

A T-Rex would make a nice friendly pet and I could take it for walks.

 → Smiffy

Kim Basincleaner

I bet Kim couldn't wait to meet me!

 Plug

The thoughts of Cuthbert Cringeworthy

Smiffy

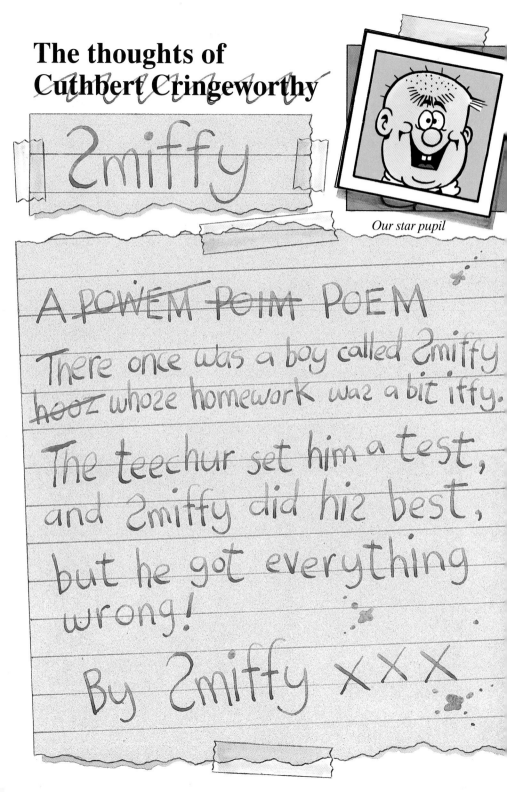

Our star pupil

A ~~POWEM~~ ~~POIM~~ POEM

There once was a boy called Smiffy
~~hooz~~ whoze homework waz a bit iffy.

The teechur set him a test,
and Smiffy did hiz best,
but he got everything wrong!

By Smiffy XXX

Pupils' report cards

The academic abilities of our pupils here at Bash Street School, leave us lost for words… but we are justly proud of our star pupil, Cuthbert Cringeworthy, whose excellent report we display below.

Cuthbert is a big girlie swot and I hate him, says Teecher.

Name:	Cuthbert Cringeworthy
Class:	Top of class II B
Report written by:	His beloved Teacher
Favourite subject:	Making his beloved Teacher happy.

Subjects:

Art:	A++
Maths:	A++
Spelling:	A++
History:	A++
Geography:	A++
Crawling:	A++++++
Knitting:	A++
Everything else:	A++

swotty Pants

Additional comments:

Cuthbert is my star pupil, and a delight to teach. Perfection is too brief a word to describe Cuthbert's many gifts. He is without doubt a future Prime Minister, a scientist or artist. Perhaps all three? Cuthbert is a genius we should all be greatly privileged to meet at least once in a lifetime.

Cuthbert is rubbish!

Name:	Smiffy
Class:	II B
Report written by:	Teacher
Favourite subject:	Playtime

Subjects:		
	Art:	Z
	Maths:	Z
	Spelling:	Z
	History:	Z
	Geography:	He couldn't even find the test paper !

Additional comments: ~~Smiffy is a complete thicky. He is so stupid that he doesn't even know just how stupid he actually is because he's usually asleep when I'm shouting at him.~~

Smiffy is a very bright boy ! ☆

Name:	Plug
Class:	II B
Report written by:	Teecher
Favourite subject:	Games

Subjects: Dead good at everything.

Additional comments: A very clever boy, and so good-looking !

Teacher's page

Dear Friends,

At last you reach the highlight of this uniquely appalling yearbook. Welcome to *my* page! The kids didn't want to let me speak to you in this way, but I threatened to cancel playtime forever. Reluctantly they agreed to let me voice my thoughts on world peace, the environment, and biscuits.

I have kept many of my all-time favourite biscuits as souvenirs. The photograph opposite shows me eating my very first chocolate biscuit.

My favourites are choccy biccies, because when you dunk them in tea, the chocolate melts and the tea tastes even better.

My worst ever experience of a biscuit was in 1957. A chocolate finger fell down the back of the settee and I didn't find it for three months! When I did eventually find it, it was in a terrible state. The chocolate had melted, it was slightly crushed and it was covered in green mould. I was heartbroken – what a terrible thing to happen to a biscuit!

Actually, when you think about it, world peace and the environment are a little like biscuits.

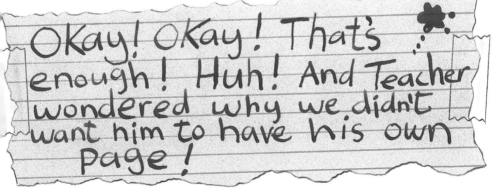

Okay! Okay! That's enough! Huh! And Teacher wondered why we didn't want him to have his own page!

School awards

Every year, Bash Street School presents awards called BASHTAs to its best pupils and staff.

Most Promising Pupil
Cuthbert Cringeworthy *CREEP*

Dinner Lady of the Year
Olive

Ugliest Pupil
Toots *(only joking, it was Plug!)*

Fattest Pupil
Fatty *(surprise, surprise!)*

Favourite Teacher
Teacher *(chosen by Headmaster)*

Favourite Headmaster
Headmaster *(chosen by Teacher)*

Join-the-Dots Champion
Spotty

Largest Collection of Jerseys
Wilfrid

Sportsman of the Year
Danny

Janitor's Cat of the Year
Winston *(as usual)*

  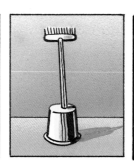

Janitor of the Year
The Janitor

Teacher's Pet of the Year
Cuthbert

Daftest excuse for missing homework

Smiffy (*"I was taken to another planet by alien brain-eating zombies who made me hand over my homework and tell them everything I knew. I was five minutes late for school too!"*)

Smiffy doesn't get an award. He won the same one last year but lost it.

Food, glorious food

Hello! I'm Olive the dinner lady. Now, the kind Headmaster has said I can have my very own page in this yearbook, to tell you all about my favourite recipes.

My dinners are like sick!

JUNK FOOD CASSEROLE:

Ingredients:

Five old prams
Six mixed socks
Ten-year-old tomato sauce
Meat (optional)

Method:

Stir gently in large cauldron until everything bubbles.
If there's any gravy left over, you can sell it to oil companies to make unleaded petrol.

MULLIGATAWNY SOUP:

Ingredients:

Curry soup
Mayonnaise

Method:

Put anything you want into a pan with two pints of water, and four tins of curry powder (just enough to kill the taste of old wellies).

Olive's a rotten cook, but her custard makes good glue!

The School nativity play

The traditional Bash Street nativity play is on the last day of school before Christmas. The kids *try* to follow the story but for some reason our Three Wise Men ride motorbikes, not camels. Last year's play was very special because, for the first time ever, it was merely a complete disaster.

THEATRE CORRESPONDENT

This photograph was taken before the rope that was holding Fatty broke.

Talent, wherefore art thou?

The kids hate doing school plays because their Teacher (that's me!) never lets them do anything that involves flamethrowers, tanks or stink bombs. I always choose a play that Cuthbert likes – just to annoy the rest of the kids.

This year I chose *Romeo and Juliet*, starring Plug and 'Erbert. I told the kids to learn something from the play. They did. The play gave them the idea to try and poison the audience with Olive's tea!

This photo shows Plug and 'Erbert performing the famous balcony scene. Originally, Fatty wanted to play Juliet, but we couldn't build a balcony strong enough.

So that's why the plays are always soppy ones, eh!

BASH STREET JOKES

What do you call a teacher who's rubbish at being a teacher?
A headmaster!

How many teechers does it take to change a lightbulb?

Three. One to change the lightbulb, one to show the headmaster how clever he is, and the third to get his class to write a story about a day in the life of a lightbulb.

Whot did Teechur zay when he ran out of ~~bizcitz~~ biscuits?

Oh, dear, I've run out of biscuits!

(We know the joke's rotten - Smiffy made it up.)

What's the best thing about school?
The holidays!

Which is the odd one out?
A teacher, a doctor, an engineer and a firefighter?
A teacher, all the rest are proper jobs!

Why did Teecher run across the road? — Because the Bash Street kids were chasing him!

What do you call something more intelligent than Teacher?
A hamster!

What's worse than Olive's school dinners?
Eating them!

What do you get if you cross a gnat's brain with a chimp?
Teacher!

Easter in the Alps

Like many fashion-conscious trendsetters, we often spend our Easter holidays skiing in Austria. Sadly, no one told the fashion-conscious trendsetters the Bash Street Kids would be there.

The rich and famous go there to ski, but we go there to roll Easter eggs down the highest mountains in Europe.

One of our favourite Alpine pastimes is rolling painted eggs down Mont Blanc. The kids paint their faces on the eggs, even Plug whose egg always shatters.

Unfortunately, the kids got bored rolling eggs down the mountain, so they rolled Cuthbert down instead.

Culture for kids

Our pupils love going to museums, art galleries and folk dancing contests. In fact, they love anything cultural!

They loved the museum... *Teacher should be in a museum!*

they couldn't wait to see the art gallery...

and I've never seen them so quiet as they were at the classical music concert. *Yawn!*

The School sports day

This year, rather than a typical sports day, we decided to hold our own Bash Street Highland Games. The mayor came along and was enjoying himself – until he was accidentally knocked out.

Fatty brought his own caber to the games.

Plug won the welly-throwing contest.

Good shot!↗

The haggis-eating competition was won by Fatty.

He was welcome to them. YUK!

We wouldn't let the kids use real hammers, only rubber ones, but they seemed to enjoy throwing them all the same.

What we did in the summer

This is how we all relaxed, away from the daily grind of learning.

Danny
I climbed Mount Everest blindfolded.

Fatty
*I spent five weeks working in a bakery.
They had to widen the door so I could leave.*

Smiffy
I didn't know it was summer!

TWIT !

Cuthbert
I spent the whole summer in the library doing extra-special homework. It was wonderful.

SWOT

Sidney
I showed Toots who was best!

Toots
I showed Sidney who was best!

'Erbert
I played computer games.

Teacher

Relaxing in the sun, I forgot about those horrible kids.

Spotty

I went mountain biking in Holland.

Wilfrid

I put compost on my head to help me grow a neck.

Plug

I was in Paris modelling the latest fashions.

Headmaster

I started writing my novel: The adventures of the beloved Headmaster.

Hopeless

Janitor & Winston

We had a great time with the kids away on holiday!

Olive

I learned more recipes.

OH, NO!!

Favourite excuses

Look what I found in my desk when I was tidying up! Did the kids really think I would be fooled by any of these notes?

YES!

I'm a thicky, and I've got this paper to prove it!

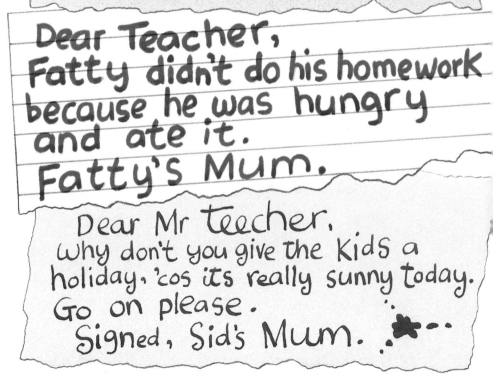

deer Teecher,
Smiffy can't do P.E. today 'cos my his legs have fallen off.
Yours Zincerely
Zmiffy's Mum. xxx

Dear Teacher,
Fatty didn't do his homework because he was hungry and ate it.
Fatty's Mum.

Dear Mr teecher.
Why don't you give the kids a holiday, 'cos its really sunny today. Go on please.
Signed, Sid's Mum.

Dear Sir
You won't see your star pupil, Cuthbert, ever again unless you make him do all the homework for all the kids in the class (especially Danny's)
Yours threateningly
Cuthbert's Dad.

Two extra pints of milk and a yogurt please, milkman.

Mrs Smiffy.

Dear Headmaster,
Teacher can't come to school today 'cos he's locked himself in a cupboard and said he's not coming back untill class IIB have been sent home.
Mrs Teacher.

Dear Mr Teacher, sir.
'Erbert wasn't at school yesterday. Well he was, he just went to the wrong one. He should be back with you as soon as his glasses have been mended.
'Erbert's Mum.

they're all true!

The School orchestra's benefit concert

In aid of the Headmaster's retirement home and hearing aid. *His brain has already retired!*

As everyone knows, music is very important to us here at Bash Street School, so what better way to raise money for a home for beloved ex-Headmasters than through the simple beauty of music. This year, our famous orchestra joined with Posh Hill School for an outstanding gala performance.

Cuthbert's prize-winning poem

I'm rubbish I am!

My beloved Teacher – the main inspiration in my life – told me that this poem is the best he's ever read. He insisted that it was included in this yearbook. Humbly, I agreed. I now dedicate this poem to my Teacher.

As a golden rule, I love my school,
Especially my beloved Teacher.
I'm never late passing through that gate,
To sit in class, I just can't wait!
The rest of IIb aren't so cool,
They just think that I'm a fool. ← Dead right
I work so hard and must endeavour,
To be so very extra-super-clever.
Plug and Danny, they may drool,
Enough to fill a swimming pool!
But I'm too clever, and I'll never, ever,
Let my right answers ever be bought.
So, though my nerves may be often fraught,
If by an ink bomb I am caught,
I know that learning can be cruel.
But that is why I love my school.
Yuk! I feel SICK!

TEACHER'S REPORT CARD

Teacher doesn't know this, but we found his old skool report card, and a picture of him when he was younger.

Name:	Teacher
Class:	II B
Report written by:	Teacher's Teacher
Favourite subject:	Misbehaving

Subjects:

Art:	F
Maths:	F
Spelling:	D
History:	E
Geography:	C
English:	D

Additional comments:

Teacher is probably the laziest, cheekiest, most badly behaved pupil I have ever had the misfortune to teach. If he had a single brain cell I would be surprised. In fact he is so hopelessly incompetent, the only career he should consider is teaching.
I just hope I never meet his pupils.

Plug's report of The Bash Street Kids on tour

Well, love us or hate us
(and everyone loves *me*),
the Bash Street Kids are always
popular visitors to foreign
countries, and we're always
keen to try new things.

*We learned first aid in no time
at all…*

*The Americans loved us. They wanted us to
stay, but we couldn't really.*

*Our first aid was quite useful when
we went mountaineering!*

We had a great time in the Caribbean.

Fatty got us thrown out of Paris.

In Africa we showed a lion who was boss.

And Australia was best of all!

But after all that, it was great to get home again!

Cuthbert's world of knitting

I know I'm not the only person who enjoys knitting trendy cardigans for their Teacher, so here is one of my favourite patterns:

Hey, the headmaster says he's really clever and NEVER makes mistakes. But does he? Look what we found in his wastepaper basket!

"Friends, readers, countriemen. Welcom to a yeer in the life of our lovible young chumms the Bash Street Kidz. They are all reelly clever and nevver do anything wrong. Cuthbert maks all the trouble."

Luv,

The Hedmaster

Bash Street disco dancing competition

Smiffy was by far the best disco party animal on the night and, exhibiting some amazing moves and funky action, he partied on down to some kickin' sounds. Dude!

Strike a pose!

Work that body!

Move to that crazy beat, man!

Get up and get busy!

Unfortunately, Smiffy didn't realise he was in a competition. All that had happened was a spider had fallen down his back!

Art competition

Every year we hold a special competition to see who can paint the best picture of their favourite teacher. For some reason last year's winner, Cuthbert Cringeworthy, did not enter a painting. He claims that someone stole it and posted it to Australia. But who would want to do a thing like that?

Hee, Hee, Hee!

I, Teacher, graciously agreed to pose, and chose the winner.

Danny's entry

Smiffy's entry

Spotty's entry

Wilfrid's entry

Toots's entry

Sidney's entry

Plug's entry

Fatty's entry

The winning entry by 'Erbert

'Erbert's so short-sighted he couldn't see that he didn't have any paint… and no-one told him until he'd finished!

Cuthbert's prize-winning ~~essay~~ DRIVEL

"The Brave, Fearless Teacher"
by Cuthbert Cringeworthy

Once upon a time in a faraway land full of fairies, pixies and pretty flowers, there lived a wise Teacher. He was also a very brave and fearless Teacher who slayed evil dragons, rescued beautiful princesses from wicked step-mothers, and taught hard sums to naughty children.

With his handsome assistant, the brave Sir Cuthbert, they travelled through their land collecting wild flowers, making scrap books, and singing happy songs. Then one day, a dark shadow fell across their happy land as an evil swarm of robbers, thieves and cads called the Bash Street Knights descended from the Mountains of Doom. The evil knights terrorised peaceful villages, robbed innocent people and only one man could stop them: the brave, fearless Teacher! At once, the brave, fearless, apple-loving Teacher set out with handsome Sir Cuthbert to collect more postage stamps for their album and crush the evil—

WIMP! Softy
Swot BIG GIRLIE!

Bash Street's winter wonderland

No decision on this year's ice sculpture competition as it went horribly wrong. *No it didn't!*

Parents' night

Parents' night is the special evening of the year when we invite parents to the school and tell them how their children are progressing. Unfortunately, the children mysteriously forgot to tell their parents about our special evening. Only Mr and Mrs Cringeworthy turned up. But never mind – it meant we had even more tea and biscuits to ourselves!

Tour de Bash Street

This is our annual school cycle race, the 'Tour de Bash Street'. In it, the kids cycle all over Beanotown. This race should not be confused with the 24-hour go-kart race, 'Le Bash Street'. Teacher kindly agreed to take action pictures of the kids racing.

Danny came first but was disqualified because his name wasn't 'Cuthbert'.

There isn't a picture of the winner receiving the trophy because this photograph was the last one taken before Teacher had to go to hospital.

He should be more careful and look before he crosses the road. Ha, Ha!

Bash Street v Posh Hill gymnastics competition

Every year Posh Hill challenge us to a gymnastics competition. For once we almost won without cheating, until Fatty remembered he was hungry!

Huh! So what's new!

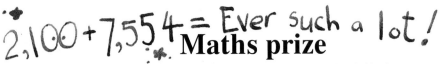
$2,100 + 7,554 =$ Ever such a lot!

Maths prize

Pre-tournament favourite Cuthbert Cringeworthy failed to turn up for the competition. Apparently, he caught something nasty that could only be cured by being shut in a dark cupboard. Smiffy claimed the prize after a breathtaking and explosive display of genius.

Smiffy goes for the big one… plus one…

Exam results

Top	~~Cuthbert~~ Smiffy	100%
Second	Winston	20%
Third		15%
Fourth		10%
Fifth		5%
Sixth		1%
Seventh		·01%
Eighth		·001%
Bottom	Danny, Plug, 'Erbert, Fatty, Sidney, Toots, Wilfrid, Spotty.	
Even lower	~~Smiffy~~ Cuthbert	

Bash Street School, Bash Street, Beanotown.

Dear Friends,

      Well, I'm afraid we've reached the end of our yearbook, and there's not much more we can do except thank the Bash Street Kids for behaving so well and not spoiling this masterpiece in any way.

I would never have believed they could behave so perfectly! But if they have done anything naughty that I might not have noticed, don't worry, I'll make sure they are punished! **OOH, ER!**

I hope you enjoyed reading about our wonderful school.

Bye, bye.

The Headmaster

It was Cuthbert who... messed this book up. NOT US!

We must not spoil our yearbook.
We must not spoil our yearbook.
We must not spoil our yearbook.
We must not spoil our yearbook.
We must not spoil our yearbook.
We must not spoil our yearbook.
We must not spoil our yearbook.
We must not spoil our yearbook
We must not spoil our yearbook
We must not spoil our yearbook.
We must not spoil our yearbook.
We must not spoil our yearbook.
We must not spoil our yearbook.
We must not spoil our yearbook.
We must not spoil our yearbook.
We must not spoil our yearbook.
We must not spoil our yearbook.
We must not spoil our yearbook.
We must not spoil our yeerbok.
We must not spoil our yeerbok.
We must not spoil our yeerbok.
We must not spoil our yearbook.
We must not spoil our yearbook.
We must not spoil our yearbook
We must not spoil our yearbook.
We must not spoil our yearbook.
We must not spoil our yearbook.